Adventures

Noah and his wife think a flood
might be coming, so they have built
a big boat called the Ark. They are
sailing around the world to rescue the
animals before it starts to rain.

Let's all go on an animal adventure!

For John Etherington
S.G.

For Martha
A.P.

Reading Consultant: Prue Goodwin, Lecturer in literacy and children's books

ORCHARD BOOKS
338 Euston Road, London NW1 3BH
Orchard Books Australia
Level 17/207 Kent Street, Sydney, NSW 2000

First published in 2011
First paperback publication in 2012

ISBN 978 1 40830 555 3 (hardback)
ISBN 978 1 40830 563 8 (paperback)

A CIP catalogue record for this book is available from the British Library.

1 3 5 7 9 10 8 6 4 2 (hardback)
1 3 5 7 9 10 8 6 4 2 (paperback)

Printed in China

Orchard Books is a division of Hachette Children's Books,
an Hachette UK company.

Giant
Giraffes!

Written by Sally Grindley

Illustrated by Alex Paterson

ORCHARD BOOKS

"Look at the sign," Noah said to his wife one morning. "We've reached Africa!"
"I've always wanted to go to Africa," said Mrs Noah. "Which animals will we find there?"

Noah opened their *Big Book of Animals*.

"Elephants, lions, zebras, hippos, giraffes and lots more," said Noah.

"Let's find the giraffes first," said Mrs Noah. "I like the word *giraffe.*"

"It says they're *always* hungry and *very* tall," said Noah.

"I hope they'll fit on the Ark!" said Mrs Noah.

They went to put on their safari clothes.

Soon they were sailing up a wide
river. Suddenly Noah cried, "Stop!
I saw something!"
Mrs Noah stopped the Ark.
"There, behind that tree," said Noah.

"Would you mind standing up
straight, so that we can see you?"
Noah called out.

A long neck stretched upwards.

Two large eyes blinked at them.

"Look at that, Mrs Noah," exclaimed
Noah. "He's almost as tall as
the tree!"

"What beautiful eyes!" said
Mrs Noah. "And what a pretty
patchwork coat!"

The giraffe began to move away.

"Don't go!" cried Noah.

"We'll have to be quick to catch up with him," said Mrs Noah.

"I know. Let's use the stilts!"

"Good idea!" said Noah. He went to

find them.

"Now I will feel like a giraffe!"
Noah said.

"Well, you *are* always hungry," said
Mrs Noah. "Take this bag of onions.
Our book says giraffes like them."
Noah set off with the stilts and the
bag of onions on his back.

Noah put the stilts against a tree.

He climbed the tree, then lowered
himself onto them.

"Whoa!" he cried. "I'm *very* tall."

"Hurry, Noah!" shouted Mrs Noah.

"There are two giraffes now."

Noah set off, wobbling this way . . .

. . . wobbling that way.

"Wait for me," he called to the
giraffes. "I've got a treat for you!"

The giraffes twitched their noses.

"I knew it!" said Noah. "You're hungry!"

One of the giraffes stuck its tongue into the bag on Noah's back.

"That's it!" said Noah. "Now, follow me."

He began to walk back to the Ark, wobbling this way . . .

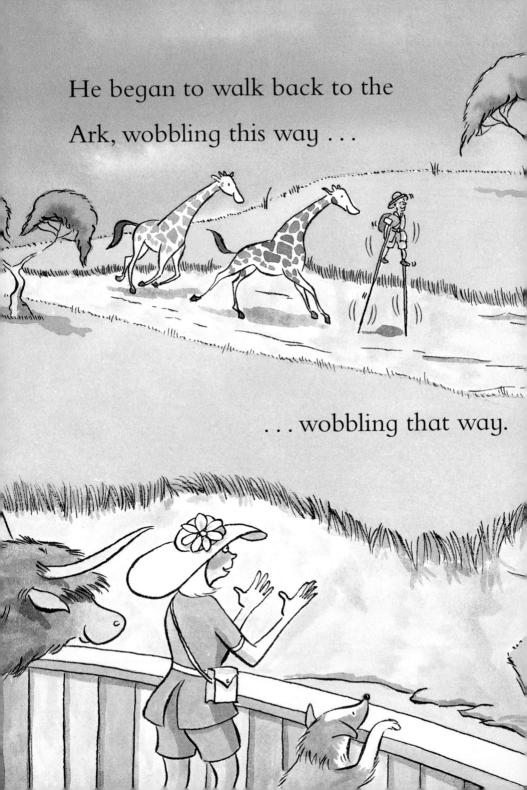

. . . wobbling that way.

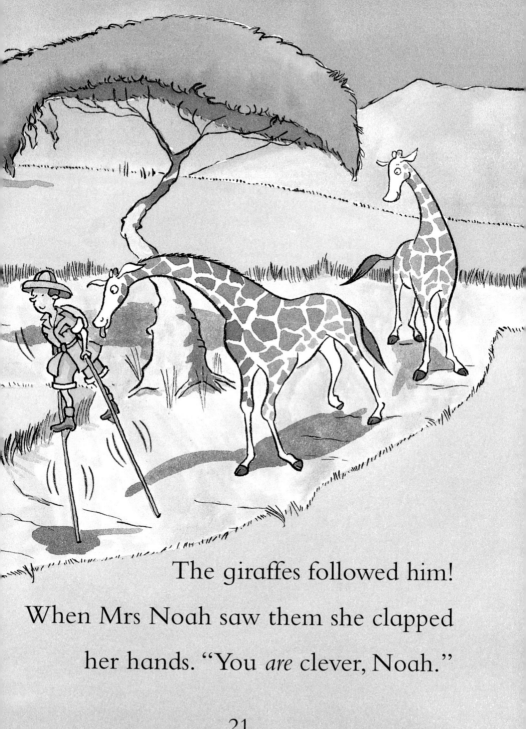

The giraffes followed him!
When Mrs Noah saw them she clapped
her hands. "You *are* clever, Noah."

The giraffes followed Noah up the gangplank. But when they reached the top, they couldn't go any further. The door to the Ark was too low!

"Try bending over," said Noah.

He bent his neck to show them how.

But the giraffes still couldn't fit

through the door!

"Wait there," said Noah.

Noah went to get a saw. He sawed the doorway to make it higher. The giraffes walked through the doorway. But inside, the ceiling was too low! "Wait there," said Noah.

Noah went up to the next deck and sawed a hole through the floor.

The giraffes popped their heads
through the hole, but they
couldn't move!

"Wait there," said Noah.

Noah sawed and sawed . . .

. . . and sawed . . .

. . . until the hole stretched from the
doorway all the way down the deck.

"There you are!" said Mrs Noah.
"I've been looking forward to
meeting you."
The giraffes twitched their noses.
"They're hungry again!" said
Noah, laughing.

Noah fetched the bag of onions.
The giraffes stuck out their long
tongues and ate noisily. Soon,
Noah's nose began to twitch.
"I think someone else is hungry,"
said Mrs Noah.

"Would you like a nice cup of tea and some cake?"

"Perfect," smiled Noah.

SALLY GRINDLEY · ALEX PATERSON

All priced at £4.99

Orchard Books are available from all good bookshops, or can be
ordered from our website: www.orchardbooks.co.uk,
or telephone 01235 827702, or fax 01235 827703.